ANDRE FREEMAN

LittyVerse

The Day the Sky Blinked

First published by UNLTD CO 2026

This novel is entirely a work of fiction. The names, characters and incidents portrayed in it are the work of the author's imagination. Any resemblance to actual persons, living or dead, events or localities is entirely coincidental.

Andre Freeman asserts the moral right to be identified as the author of this work.

First edition

ISBN (paperback): 979-8-90220-004-8
ISBN (hardcover): 979-8-90220-005-5
ISBN (digital): 979-8-90220-002-4

This book was professionally typeset on Reedsy.
Find out more at reedsy.com

"Some moments don't change the world.
world.
They reveal it."

A. FREEMAN

Contents

Acknowledgments   iii
LittyVerse: The Day the Sky Blinked A LittyVerse
Novel By...   iv

I   Part One

CHAPTER 1: THE DAY THE SKY BLINKED   3
CHAPTER 2: THE MESSAGE THAT SHOULDN'T
EXIST   7
CHAPTER 3: THE BUILDING THAT BREATHED   10
CHAPTER 4: THE WORLD DIDN'T CHANGE
— I DID   14
CHAPTER 5: THE GIRL WHO DIDN'T BLINK   18
CHAPTER 6: THE FIRST MISTAKE   22
CHAPTER 7: THEY DON'T KNOCK   25
CHAPTER 8: THE PLACE THAT DOESN'T EXIST   28
CHAPTER 9: THE FIRST RULE   31
CHAPTER 10: THE ONE YOU DON'T SAVE   34
CHAPTER 11: THE COST OF STAYING   37
CHAPTER 12: THE ONES WHO NEVER LEFT   40
CHAPTER 13: THE FIRST LIE HE DIDN'T TELL   43
CHAPTER 14: THE TEST THEY COULDN'T MEASURE   46
CHAPTER 15: WHEN A SYSTEM DECIDES   49
CHAPTER 16: THE QUIET COLLAPSE   52

CHAPTER 17: THE DOOR THEY DIDN'T CLOSE 55
CHAPTER 18: WHEN THE SKY DOESN'T BLINK 58

Notes 60
About the Author 61
Also by Andre Freeman 62

Acknowledgments

This story exists because imagination never asked for permission.

To everyone who believes in building something bigger than themselves — thank you.

And to the future creators of the LittyVerse... this is only the beginning.

I

Part One

CHAPTER 1: THE DAY THE SKY BLINKED

LITTY always knew something off about the sky. Not in the "weather app lied again" way. Not even in the "the clouds look like a dragon if you squint" way. More like the sky had a personality—one that pretended to be calm until you stared too long, and then it stared back. He noticed it most on mornings when the city was still deciding whether it wanted to be alive. The street below his apartment smelled like warm asphalt and old food wrappers.

A bus hissed at the curb like it was tired of carrying everyone's problems. A shopping cart rolled by itself down the sidewalk, wobbling like it had someplace important to be, even though it didn't. LITTY stood at the corner with his hoodie up, backpack hanging off one shoulder, and the kind of tired in his eyes that didn't come from sleep. He looked up between two cracked apartment buildings, where a slice of sky lived like a screensaver. Clouds drifted. Birds cut through the air. Everything normal. Then the clouds blinked. Not moved. Not shifted. Not drifted into a different shape.

Blinked—quick, bright, unmistakable, like an eye closing and opening. LITTY froze so hard it felt like somebody hit pause on his body. "...Nah," he muttered, rubbing his eyes with the heel of his palm. "Not doing this today." He looked down at his phone like it was going to explain reality to him. No emergency alerts. No weather warnings. No breaking news headline screaming SKY MALFUNCTION. Just a missed text from his cousin and a reminder he was late again, like the universe couldn't give him one peaceful morning without a deadline attached. He stepped off the curb—and a horn blasted loud enough to vibrate his ribs. "Yo! Watch it!" a driver yelled out the window.

LITTY jerked back, heart racing, then laughed like it was all good. Like he hadn't just watched the sky act human. That was his specialty: pretending. Pretending the streetlights didn't flicker when he walked under them. Pretending his reflection didn't sometimes smile a fraction of a second after he did. Pretending he didn't dream about places he'd never been—cities floating above oceans of light, towers wrapped in glowing chains, a voice calling his name like it had known him longer than his own mother had. LITTY. Not his real name, but the one that stuck. The one people remembered. The one that sounded like a joke until it didn't. He adjusted his hoodie and kept walking, trying to convince his body the sky blink had been a tired-brain illusion. And for about thirty seconds, it almost worked. Then the air changed. Not colder. Not hotter. Heavier. Charged. Like the moment right before lightning cracks open the world. LITTY slowed. His steps became careful without him choosing it.

The city noise—cars, music leaking from open windows, distant sirens—kept going, but it felt like it was happening through glass. Across the street, a street artist froze mid-spray. The paint mist hung in the air too long. A pigeon flapped once, then stopped, hovering like it forgot gravity. Even the bus at the curb seemed stuck between braking and moving. Time didn't stop. It hesitated. LITTY's throat went dry. "Nope," he whispered. "Nope. Not me." The clouds blinked again—brighter this time, sharper, like an eyelid snapping open fully. And in that blink, LITTY felt something lock onto him. Not a stare. A scan. Like a spotlight with intelligence. His phone vibrated in his hand so hard he almost dropped it. UNKNOWN NUMBER It's time. Don't run. His pulse slammed. LITTY turned in a slow circle, eyes searching the street like he'd catch whoever was behind it. Nobody looked at him. Nobody even flinched. People walked past like normal, laughing, talking, living their day, while LITTY stood in the middle of a city that had just betrayed its own rules. His phone vibrated again. UNKNOWN NUMBER You noticed the blink. LITTY's breath caught. He stared up at the slice of sky between buildings, and this time it didn't look peaceful. It looked like a screen covering something else. He swallowed, forcing his voice to come out steady even though his hands were shaking. "Who is this?" No typing bubble. No delay. Just an instant response, like the message had already been written. UNKNOWN NUMBER Someone who doesn't want you to hurt people. LITTY's stomach flipped. He didn't know whether to laugh or panic. He chose the third option—the one he always chose. He started walking faster, like he could outrun the feeling crawling up his spine. And the city, sensing his shift, snapped back into full motion like nothing had happened. The street artist resumed spraying. The pigeon dropped and strutted like it had never hovered. The bus pulled away, engine groaning. Normal. But LITTY knew better now. Once you see the crack, you can't unsee it. His phone buzzed one more time. UNKNOWN

NUMBER Don't go home. LITTY stopped in the middle of the sidewalk, chest rising and falling too fast. He didn't want to be special. He didn't want to be targeted. He didn't want the sky to know his name.

But the truth was already inside him, heavy as a second heartbeat: Whatever had been waiting for him—whatever had been watching— It had finally decided today was the day. And LITTY's life was about to stop being normal forever.

CHAPTER 2: THE MESSAGE THAT SHOULDN'T EXIST

LITTY didn't go home. He didn't know where he was going either — he just knew the message was right. Something in his chest had shifted the moment he read it, like a door unlocking inside his ribs. He walked fast, cutting through side streets, past murals peeling off brick walls, past alleyways that smelled like rain and old stories. The city felt louder now, but not in sound — in awareness. Like it was paying attention to him in small, invisible ways. His phone stayed warm in his hand. No new messages. But the silence felt intentional. He ducked into a small park wedged between two apartment blocks.

Half the lights were out. A broken swing creaked slowly in the breeze even though nobody touched it. LITTY sat on a bench and finally let himself breathe. "Okay," he whispered. "Okay. You noticed the sky blink. That's normal. People notice weird stuff all the time. It doesn't mean..." His phone buzzed. UNKNOWN NUMBER You're trying to talk yourself out of the truth. LITTY swallowed. "Who are you?" he typed. Three dots appeared instantly. Then vanished. Then appeared again. UNKNOWN NUMBER Someone who once tried to ignore the same thing.

LITTY's thumbs hovered. "You hacked my phone?" he typed. UNKNOWN NUMBER No. You invited me. That line made his stomach twist. "I didn't invite anything." UNKNOWN NUMBER You looked at the sky when everyone else looked down. You felt the pause when everyone else accepted the noise. You're already inside the door. You just haven't turned around yet. LITTY leaned back on the bench, staring up at the dark branches above him. "You sound crazy." UNKNOWN NUMBER So did the last person who saved a city. LITTY snorted despite himself. "You're doing too much now." UNKNOWN NUMBER I'm doing just enough. Another pause.

Then— UNKNOWN NUMBER They're watching you. LITTY's head snapped up. "Who?" UNKNOWN NUMBER The ones who don't like questions. The ones who built systems to make sure people stop asking them. LITTY's pulse climbed. "You're not helping." UNKNOWN NUMBER I'm not here to help. I'm here to prepare you. The words felt heavier than the screen. "Prepare me for what?" This time the dots stayed longer. UNKNOWN NUMBER For the moment you realize your life doesn't belong only to you anymore. A car passed nearby, headlights washing over the park for a split second. When the light faded, LITTY noticed something he hadn't before. The shadows didn't line up correctly. The tree's shadow bent slightly away from the trunk. The bench's shadow leaned in a direction no light source supported. The world wasn't broken. It was... layered. "You see it now," the message appeared. LITTY stood slowly. "Yeah," he typed. "I see something." UNKNOWN NUMBER Good. Because you're about to be asked to decide whether you want to keep pretending you don't. A new message arrived immediately after. UNKNOWN NUMBER There's a building three blocks east of you. Old medical facility. Looks abandoned. It isn't. LITTY's heart pounded. "No." UNKNOWN NUMBER You're going. LITTY shook his head. "You don't get to tell me what I'm doing." UNKNOWN NUMBER I don't. But the people inside that building already have. LITTY stared at the dark path leading out of the park. "Why me?" he typed. This time, the reply took longer. UNKNOWN NUMBER Because you're not empty. Because you're not numb. Because you don't turn away when something hurts. And because when the sky blinked, you didn't laugh. You listened. LITTY's chest tightened. "Who did I hurt?" he typed quietly. UNKNOWN NUMBER Not yet. But you will... if you don't learn what you are. The wind shifted. The broken swing creaked louder. LITTY felt the world press closer around him. "What am I?" The reply came slower. He could feel the weight behind it. UNKNOWN NUMBER A bridge. Between what people are... And what they're being forced to become. LITTY exhaled. "This is insane." UNKNOWN NUMBER Yes. But it's real. Another message followed. UNKNOWN NUMBER You can walk away. You'll still live. You'll still laugh. You'll still eat, sleep, love, and forget.

But somewhere, someone will carry what you could have helped hold. And one day, you'll feel the weight of that choice without knowing why. LITTY closed his eyes. He thought about the blinking sky. The frozen pigeon. The hanging paint mist. The feeling that the world had hesitated for him. He opened his eyes. "Which way is the building?" he typed. Three dots. Then— UNKNOWN NUMBER Good. Turn right. And don't look back. LITTY stood up. For the first time in his life, he wasn't late for anything. He was early. And the world, finally, was waiting for him. —-

CHAPTER 3: THE BUILDING THAT BREATHED

The building didn't look abandoned. It looked forgotten. Its windows were dark but not broken. Its doors were sealed, but not rusted shut. The walls were too clean for something that hadn't been touched in years. Even the graffiti felt... hesitant. Like whoever sprayed it had second-guessed the act. LITTY stopped across the street. The air felt heavier here. Not thicker — heavier. Like gravity had increased by one invisible degree. He checked his phone. No messages. But he didn't need one. He already knew this was the place.

A faded sign above the entrance still read: NORTHRIDGE MEDICAL RESEARCH The word *research* felt louder than the rest. LITTY crossed the street. Each step echoed too clearly. He placed his hand on the door. It opened. No resistance. No creak. No alarm. The air inside was cool and clean, like a hospital that never learned how to age. Lights flickered to life one by one down the hallway. Not suddenly. Not dramatically. Gently. Like the building was waking up. LITTY froze. "Okay," he whispered. "Okay. I'm officially in a horror movie." His footsteps echoed down polished floors. Doors lined both sides — labeled with words he didn't fully understand. OBSERVATION.

CONDITIONING. RESPONSE. MEMORY. He felt watched. Not by cameras. By awareness. He reached the end of the hall. A single door waited. No label. Just a fingerprint scanner glowing faint blue. LITTY stared at it. "Yeah, no," he muttered. His phone buzzed. UNKNOWN NUMBER You don't need to touch it. He stepped back. The scanner pulsed. Then turned green. The door opened. Inside wasn't a room. It was a chamber. Circular. White walls. Soft light. No visible ceiling. The floor felt slightly warm beneath his shoes. And in the center... A platform. Floating. Not attached to anything. Suspended by nothing. LITTY's breath caught. The platform lowered slowly until it hovered just inches above the floor. On it sat a single object. A mirror. But not glass. Liquid. The surface rippled like water, but reflected perfectly.

LITTY approached slowly. He looked into it. At first, he saw himself. Then he didn't. The reflection lagged behind his movements. His real self lifted a hand. The reflection waited a half second longer. Then lifted its own. The reflection smiled. LITTY hadn't. He stumbled back. "What the—" The reflection spoke. Not out loud. Inside his head. **You finally arrived.** LITTY clutched his temples. "I'm losing it." **No. You're waking up.** The reflection stepped forward. Out of the mirror. Onto the platform. Onto the floor. Now there were two of him. Same face. Same clothes. Different eyes. The reflection's eyes glowed faintly silver. "You're not real," LITTY whispered. The other LITTY tilted his head. **Define real.** The walls pulsed softly.

LITTY backed away until he felt the wall behind him. "Why me?" he demanded again. The other LITTY walked slowly around him, studying him like an experiment. **Because you don't belong to any system completely.** "You don't know me." **I know you better than you know yourself.** He stopped in front of LITTY. **You were born between expectations. You learned to survive between definitions. You learned to see between rules.** LITTY's throat tightened. "You're just saying words." **Words are the only things that cross dimensions without permission.** The other LITTY raised a hand. The room shifted. Suddenly the walls became memories.

LITTY saw himself as a kid. Sitting alone. Watching others fit in while he hovered just outside belonging. He saw arguments. Moves. Losses. Dreams. Attempts. Failures. Resets. "You're showing me my life," LITTY whispered. **No. I'm showing you your pattern.** The images sped up. LITTY saw himself questioning everything. Never settling. Never fully accepting the surface. **You are not broken,** the reflection said. **You are unassigned.** The memories faded. The room returned. "What does that even mean?" LITTY asked. **It means the world cannot place you.** The reflection stepped closer. **Which means you can move through it differently.** LITTY shook his head. "I didn't ask for this." **Neither did gravity.** **Neither did time.** **Neither did truth.** The reflection placed two fingers against LITTY's chest. LITTY gasped. Not in pain. In expansion. He felt something unlock inside him — not like a power turning on, but like a wall stepping aside. He could feel the building. The city. The electrical lines. The emotions of distant people. The hum of existence. He pulled away, breathing hard. "What did you just do to me?" The reflection smiled softly. **I removed a filter.** LITTY collapsed onto the floor. His heart pounded like thunder. "You can't just change me." **I didn't change you.** **I reminded you.** The reflection walked back toward the mirror. **They will come for you now.** "Who?" **The ones who need everyone asleep.** "Can I undo this?" The reflection stopped at the mirror. **No.** **But you can decide what you become.** The reflection stepped backward. Merged into the liquid mirror. The platform slowly rose back into the ceiling. The room lights dimmed. The door behind LITTY opened. UNKNOWN NUMBER appeared on his phone. UNKNOWN NUMBER You survived the first door.

LITTY stood slowly. "I don't feel the same," he typed. UN-KNOWN NUMBER You're not. Welcome to the part of your life that can't be taken away. LITTY walked out of the building. The night felt brighter. The city felt louder. The world felt thinner. He looked up at the sky. It didn't blink. It watched. And for the first time... LITTY knew the sky was watching back.

CHAPTER 4: THE WORLD DIDN'T CHANGE — I DID

LITTY didn't realize how different he felt until he tried to walk like nothing had happened. His legs moved, but his balance felt... recalibrated. Like gravity had shifted its rules slightly when he wasn't looking. The streetlights looked sharper. The colors deeper. The sounds layered — footsteps, distant laughter, engines, wind — all stacked instead of blended. The world hadn't changed. He had. He stopped on the sidewalk, placing a hand against a brick wall just to steady himself. It was warm.

Not from the sun. From energy. He could feel it. The wall wasn't dead. The air wasn't empty. Even silence wasn't silent anymore. "Okay," he whispered. "Okay, okay, okay..." A couple walked past him, laughing, completely unaware that the universe had just rewritten its relationship with him. He checked his phone. No new messages. But he didn't feel alone. Not anymore. He walked. And as he walked, he started noticing things he'd never noticed before. People's emotions didn't just show on their faces — they moved around them. Some glowed heavy. Some flickered sharp. Some dragged behind like shadows that didn't want to follow. A man arguing on the phone carried a red pulse in his chest.

A woman sitting on a bus bench glowed blue and tired. A kid running past him shimmered gold for half a second. LITTY blinked. The colors didn't go away. He wasn't hallucinating. He was... interpreting. He turned down a side street and leaned against a lamppost, breathing hard. "This is too much," he whispered. His phone buzzed. UNKNOWN NUMBER You're seeing the emotional spectrum. LITTY typed fast. "You could've warned me." UNKNOWN NUMBER You wouldn't have believed me. LITTY exhaled slowly.

"What am I supposed to do with this?" UNKNOWN NUMBER That depends on whether you want to hide from it... Or learn to use it. A car passed, its headlights stretching shadows across the pavement. The shadows moved a fraction too late. LITTY noticed. "Use it how?" UNKNOWN NUMBER By realizing the world isn't controlled only by money, weapons, or laws. It's controlled by emotion. By fear. By hope. By distraction. By pain. And now... You can see where it leaks. LITTY stared at his hands. They looked normal. But he felt something moving beneath the skin — not physically, but structurally. "Am I dangerous?" he typed. The reply didn't come immediately. UNKNOWN NUMBER Not yet. That scared him more than a yes would have. He walked again, slowly this time, absorbing the city. A man bumped into him. "Watch it," the man snapped. For half a second, LITTY felt the man's anger like heat in his chest. He stepped back without thinking. "Sorry," LITTY said quietly. The man paused, confused, then waved it off and walked away.

LITTY realized something. He hadn't just sensed the anger. He had softened it. He looked at his palm. "What did I just do?" UNKNOWN NUMBER You adjusted the field. LITTY's heartbeat sped up. "So I can change people?" UNKNOWN NUMBER You can influence states. Not control. Not command. But shift. Nudge. Stabilize. Or destabilize. LITTY swallowed. "That's insane." UNKNOWN NUMBER That's responsibility. He reached a small bridge overlooking a drainage canal. Water trickled below, reflecting broken pieces of the city lights. LITTY leaned over the railing. "I didn't ask to be responsible for people." UNKNOWN NUMBER None of the ones who mattered ever did. The wind moved through his hair. LITTY felt suddenly small. And impossibly important at the same time. "What happens next?" he typed. UNKNOWN NUMBER Next, you learn restraint. Then precision. Then truth. Then you choose. "Choose what?" UNKNOWN NUMBER Who you are when no one tells you what to be. LITTY closed his eyes. He felt the city breathing. He felt the fear buried under laughter. He felt the hope buried under exhaustion. He felt the weight of a world that didn't know it was tired. When he opened his eyes, he whispered: "I don't want to be like them."

UNKNOWN NUMBER Then don't be. Be better. But don't be louder. Be clearer. LITTY looked at the reflection in the water. He still looked like himself. But behind his eyes... Something had woken up. Something patient. Something unfinished. Something that didn't belong to anyone else. He straightened. "I'm not running," he typed. UNKNOWN NUMBER Good.

Because tomorrow, you meet someone who already tried. LITTY's stomach tightened. "Meet where?" UNKNOWN NUMBER At school. LITTY froze. "...You know where I go?"

UNKNOWN NUMBER We know where everyone goes. But not everyone matters. LITTY stared at the screen. And for the first time... He didn't feel hunted. He felt chosen. He walked home under a sky that no longer blinked... Because it didn't need to. It had already opened its eyes.

CHAPTER 5: THE GIRL WHO DIDN'T BLINK

School felt wrong. Not dangerous. Not broken. Just... misaligned. Like the building existed in a slightly different layer than it had yesterday. LITTY walked through the front gates and immediately felt it. Noise without awareness. Movement without presence. Hundreds of students walking, talking, laughing, complaining — but emotionally, most of them were half-asleep. He could see it now. Colors floated around people like invisible weather. Gray boredom. Green envy. Blue sadness. Red irritation. Gold flashes that vanished too fast. He lowered his head and kept moving. UNKNOWN NUMBER Don't stare too long. You'll forget how to pretend. LITTY typed without stopping. "I already feel like I don't belong here anymore." UNKNOWN NUMBER That's the cost of seeing.

LITTY reached his locker. He opened it. Inside sat a single folded piece of black paper. Not his handwriting. Not anyone's he recognized. His heart jumped. He looked around. Nobody noticed. He unfolded it slowly. **You're late.** His phone buzzed. UNKNOWN NUMBER You weren't supposed to get that yet. "Then who gave it to me?" he typed. UNKNOWN NUMBER

Someone who doesn't listen to schedules. LITTY swallowed. He scanned the hallway again. That's when he saw her. She stood near the stairwell, leaning casually against the wall, scrolling on her phone.

Normal clothes. Normal posture. Normal expression. But her emotional color didn't match anyone else. She wasn't glowing. She wasn't flickering. She wasn't leaking emotion at all. She was... still. Like a blank space in the spectrum. She looked up. Her eyes met his. And she didn't look away. Everyone else around them moved. Talked. Passed. Ignored. But she didn't. She tilted her head slightly. Then smiled. Not friendly. Not cold. Knowing. LITTY's chest tightened. UNKNOWN NUMBER That's her. "Her who?" he typed. UNKNOWN NUMBER The one who didn't run. She pushed off the wall and walked toward him. Each step felt heavier than the last. When she stopped in front of him, she spoke before he could.

"You're breathing wrong." He blinked. "Excuse me?" "You're holding air like you're scared it might betray you." He stared. "...Do I know you?" She smirked slightly. "Not yet." She glanced at his locker. "You got the note." LITTY's heart thumped. "You wrote that?" "No." "Then who did?" She leaned closer, lowering her voice. "The building." His breath caught. She studied his face. "You went inside." It wasn't a question. LITTY whispered, "How do you know?" She tapped her temple. "Because I didn't." He felt the weight of her words. "You were supposed to," he said without knowing why. She nodded once. "Yeah." They stood in silence. Then she sighed. "Look, before your mystery friend texts you something dramatic — yes, I see what you see." LITTY stiffened. "What do you see?"

She scanned the hallway. "Emotion. Pressure. Fear patterns. Probability leaks. System seams." LITTY whispered, "You sound like you've been practicing that." She smiled faintly. "I've been waiting for someone to say it out loud." LITTY swallowed. "What's your name?" "Nova." He nodded slowly. "I'm LITTY." She laughed softly. "Yeah, I know." His eyes widened. She shrugged. "You leave fingerprints in places you don't touch." UNKNOWN NUMBER buzzed. UNKNOWN NUMBER Do not trust her too fast. LITTY typed back. "She already knows too much." UNKNOWN NUMBER Exactly. Nova watched his phone. "You can tell them I said hi." LITTY froze.

"You can see my messages?" "No," she said calmly. "But I can hear your pauses." She stepped closer. "You're not the first one who woke up." His stomach dropped. "How many are there?" She looked away. "Not enough." "And the others?" She met his eyes again. "Most of them disappeared." The bell rang. Students surged around them. But LITTY and Nova didn't move. "Why didn't you disappear?" he asked. She smiled, but it didn't reach her eyes. "Because I broke the rules before they finished writing them." LITTY felt something shift inside him. Not fear. Alignment. "You're not here to save me," he said. "No," she replied softly. "I'm here to make sure you don't save the wrong people." LITTY's chest tightened. She turned and started walking away. Then stopped. "Oh — and LITTY?" "Yeah?" She looked back. "The sky didn't blink for you alone." She walked into the crowd and vanished. UNKNOWN NUMBER buzzed.

UNKNOWN NUMBER You've just met your contradiction. LITTY exhaled slowly. "Is that bad?" UNKNOWN NUMBER It means your story just stopped being safe. LITTY closed his locker. And for the first time... He felt like he wasn't the only one standing on the edge of something impossible.

CHAPTER 6: THE FIRST MISTAKE

LITTY didn't realize he was smiling until Nova disappeared. Not because he was happy. Because he finally felt seen. That was the problem. He walked to class with his head full and his chest tight. The colors around people pulsed stronger now, like his awareness had sharpened just from talking to her. He slid into his seat near the back of the room. The teacher started talking. LITTY heard none of it. He kept replaying Nova's words. "You're not the first one who woke up." He felt something shift in his chest again. UNKNOWN NUMBER buzzed. UNKNOWN NUMBER Do not let connection make you careless.

"I didn't do anything," he typed. UNKNOWN NUMBER You're about to. LITTY frowned. Before he could respond, a girl two rows ahead suddenly slammed her notebook shut. "I can't do this anymore," she muttered. Her emotional color exploded — red, blue, black tangled together. The room didn't notice. But LITTY did. He felt it like a storm in his ribs. Her pain wasn't loud. It was compressed. Dangerously. She stood abruptly and walked toward the door. The teacher called after her. She didn't answer. LITTY watched her leave. And without thinking...

He reached. Not physically. Emotionally. He focused on her fear and imagined it loosening. Softening. Breathing. The hallway light flickered. The girl stopped walking. She turned around slowly. Her shoulders dropped. Her breathing steadied. She wiped her face, then quietly returned to her seat. The class continued like nothing happened. LITTY's hands trembled. "What did I just do?" he whispered. UNKNOWN NUMBER buzzed immediately. UNKNOWN NUMBER You interfered. LITTY typed fast. "She was breaking." UNKNOWN NUMBER And now the system knows you exist.

His stomach dropped. Across the room, Nova slowly turned in her seat. She looked at him. Not surprised. Concerned. She shook her head once. Very slightly. LITTY swallowed. The rest of the class passed in a blur. When the bell rang, Nova stood and walked straight to him. "Outside," she said quietly. They walked behind the gym, where no one usually went. Nova crossed her arms. "You pushed emotion," she said. "I helped her." "You changed a trajectory." "She was about to fall apart." Nova exhaled slowly. "Do you know how many people fall apart every day?" LITTY looked down. "No." "Exactly." She stepped closer. "You don't fix storms by redirecting lightning. You learn how storms work first." LITTY clenched his jaw. "So I should've just watched?" "No," Nova said softly. "You should've felt." "You should've learned." "You should've waited." He looked at her. Her eyes softened. "I made the same mistake." "What happened?" She hesitated. "Someone else paid for it." LITTY's chest tightened. UNKNOWN NUMBER buzzed.

UNKNOWN NUMBER The first use always feels righteous. The second feels necessary. The third feels justified. After that, you forget to ask why. LITTY whispered, "I didn't mean to start anything." Nova looked past him, toward the school. "You didn't start it," she said. "You stepped into it." A low hum passed through the air. Not a sound. A pressure. LITTY felt it in his teeth. Nova stiffened. "They felt that," she said. "Who?" "The watchers." His stomach turned. "They already know me?" "They knew you when you touched the mirror," she said. "But now…" She looked back at him. "…they know you'll act." LITTY whispered, "Am I in danger?" Nova shook her head. "No." "You're in demand." He laughed nervously. "That's worse." She gave a small, serious smile. "Welcome to the part where they stop ignoring you." UNKNOWN NUMBER buzzed again. UNKNOWN NUMBER You did not fail.

But you have now declared intent. "What does that mean?" LITTY typed. UNKNOWN NUMBER It means your story is no longer optional. LITTY felt the weight of that sentence settle inside him. Nova stepped back. "We're not heroes," she said. "We're variables." LITTY looked at his hands. They still looked normal. But he knew better now. He wasn't a background character anymore. He had touched the story.

And the story had touched back. Above them, clouds shifted unnaturally. LITTY looked up. The sky didn't blink. It focused.

CHAPTER 7: THEY DON'T KNOCK

The message came while LITTY was pretending to do homework. His notebook was open. His pen rested on the page. None of the words mattered. His phone vibrated once. Not a buzz. A tap. Like a knuckle against glass. UNKNOWN NUMBER They are coming tonight. LITTY's breath caught. "How do you know?" he typed. UNKNOWN NUMBER Because they already asked me if you were ready. His chest tightened. "Asked you how?" Three dots appeared. Disappeared. Reappeared. UNKNOWN NUMBER By turning off a city block. LITTY stood slowly and walked to his window. Outside, the streetlights at the end of the block were dark. Not broken. Not flickering. Just... gone.

The rest of the street still glowed. A clean cut. Nova's voice echoed in his head. *You're in demand.* LITTY typed with shaking thumbs. "What do they want?" UNKNOWN NUMBER To decide what you are. LITTY whispered, "I already decided." UNKNOWN NUMBER They don't care. A knock hit his door. Not loud. Not aggressive. Perfectly timed. LITTY froze. His heartbeat slammed in his ears.

The knock came again. Three soft taps. He didn't move. His

phone vibrated. UNKNOWN NUMBER Do not open it. The door handle turned anyway. Slowly. Deliberately. The door opened. Two people stood in the hallway. Not in black suits. Not in uniforms. They wore simple clothes. Calm faces. Neutral posture. Human. Which made it worse. "LITTY," the woman said gently. "We just want to talk." His body felt locked. The man beside her studied him with quiet interest. "You felt the shift today," the man said. "You interfered." LITTY swallowed. "She was hurting." The woman nodded. "We know." "That's why we're here." They stepped inside without asking.

The door closed behind them. LITTY backed up until he felt the edge of his bed. "You can't just—" "We can," the man said calmly. "We just don't like to scare people." The woman looked around his room. Posters. Shoes. Books. Normal. "You're younger than we expected," she said. LITTY clenched his fists. "What are you?" The man smiled slightly. "Custodians." "Of what?" "Balance." LITTY laughed once, nervous. "You sound like villains in a bad movie." The woman tilted her head. "We sound like people who clean up what others destabilize." The air in the room thickened. Not hot. Not cold. Heavy. LITTY felt his chest tighten. Nova was right.

This was what pressure felt like. "You touched emotional infrastructure today," the man said. "You redirected it." LITTY shook his head. "I just helped her breathe." The woman nodded. "And in doing so, you changed three probability threads." His stomach dropped. "You track people's feelings?" "We track outcomes," she replied. "Feelings are just the ignition." LITTY whispered, "So what now?" They looked at each other briefly. Then back at him. "Now we decide if you're a risk..." "...or a resource." LITTY felt something in his spine tighten — not explode, not surge — align. "I'm not either," he said quietly. The man raised an eyebrow. "Everyone is one of the two." "No," LITTY said. "I'm a person." The woman studied him for a long moment. Then smiled faintly. "That answer is why we didn't bring restraints." The man stepped closer. "You have two options," he said. "You come with us for evaluation..." "...or you stay here and we escalate the situation until you have no choice." LITTY's phone vibrated in his pocket. UNKNOWN NUMBER This is the moment.

Nova's words echoed. *We're variables.* LITTY lifted his head. "Where would you take me?" The woman answered. "To a place that will either protect you..." "...or erase you." Silence filled the room. LITTY exhaled slowly. "Can I say goodbye to someone?" The man smiled politely. "You just did." The lights in the room dimmed. The walls hummed softly. And the world LITTY thought he understood began folding into something much bigger.

He stepped forward. Not because he was ready. But because he refused to run.

CHAPTER 8: THE PLACE THAT DOESN'T EXIST

They didn't put a hood over his head. That was the first lie. They didn't restrain him. That was the second. They simply walked him out of his room, down the stairs, past neighbors who didn't look up, into a plain black vehicle that didn't reflect streetlights correctly. The woman opened the door for him. "Comfort matters," she said kindly. LITTY didn't answer. He slid into the back seat. The door closed with a soft, airtight click. The inside smelled clean. Not new. Not old. Neutral. The city began to move past the windows — streets, lights, people — but the motion felt slightly delayed, like the car was traveling through a version of the world that lagged behind the real one.

LITTY leaned forward. "We're not on the highway," he said. The man in the passenger seat glanced at him in the mirror. "No," he replied. "We're between routes." LITTY swallowed. The hum beneath the car deepened. The lights outside blurred into smooth ribbons instead of passing shapes. LITTY felt pressure in his ears, like an airplane climbing too fast. "You're not driving," LITTY said. The woman smiled softly. "No. We're arriving." The city vanished. Not faded. Not cut. Simply... replaced. Outside the windows now stretched a vast, dark expanse broken by distant structures that looked like glass folded into impossible shapes. Towers without windows. Bridges without supports. Platforms floating where ground should have been. LITTY's breath caught. "Where are we?" The man answered quietly. "Nowhere officially." The car slowed and stopped beside a wide entrance carved into a black wall that reflected nothing. The door opened. Cold, clean air washed over LITTY's face. He stepped out. The ground beneath his shoes was smooth and slightly warm, like it remembered footsteps.

Above him, the ceiling wasn't a ceiling. It was depth. Layers of light suspended in slow motion. "We call this facility Meridian," the woman said. LITTY whispered, "It's underground." The man shook his head. "It's under permission." They led him forward. Doors opened as they approached. Not sliding. Unfolding. Inside, corridors curved gently, like the building was shaped by water instead of design. People moved through the halls. Not many. But enough. Some wore uniforms. Some wore casual clothes. Some looked like students. Some looked like ghosts who forgot how to leave. LITTY felt it. He wasn't alone here. He never had been. They stopped before a transparent wall. Behind it, a boy about LITTY's age sat on a bench, staring at his hands. His emotional color was fractured — sharp flashes of red and violet breaking apart before they could form.

The boy looked up. Their eyes met. Recognition passed between them instantly. Not memory. Kinship. "He woke up like you," the woman said quietly. "What happened to him?" LITTY asked. The man replied, "He didn't listen." LITTY's stomach tightened. They walked again. They passed a room where a girl sat in total silence, eyes open but distant. Another where someone whispered to themselves in repeating patterns. Another where laughter echoed with no one inside. LITTY stopped walking. "You said you protect people," he said. "We do," the woman replied. "From themselves." "And from what they could become," the man added. LITTY whispered, "This isn't protection. This is containment." They didn't argue. They led him into a room. Not small. Not large. Just enough.

A bed. A table. A window that showed nothing but light. "This is your room," the woman said. "You'll rest." "You'll learn." "You'll be evaluated." LITTY looked at her. "And if I fail?" She paused. "You won't," she said gently. But her emotional color flickered. Just for a second. The door closed behind them. Softly. Not locked. But sealed. LITTY stood alone in the center of the room. He felt it now. The truth. He wasn't the first. He wasn't unique. He wasn't chosen. He was cataloged. He sat on the edge of the bed and exhaled slowly.

His phone vibrated. UNKNOWN NUMBER You're inside. LITTY typed. "Where are you?" UNKNOWN NUMBER Outside the system. And trying to pull you back out. LITTY closed his eyes. He felt the walls. The layers. The watching. The waiting. He whispered to himself: "I'm not disappearing in here." And for the first time since the sky blinked... He realized the real story wasn't about discovering his power. It was about surviving the place built to own it.

CHAPTER 9: THE FIRST RULE

T he room never went dark. That was the first thing LITTY noticed. No night. No dim. No off. Just a soft, constant light that made time feel optional. He lay on the bed staring at the ceiling, trying to count breaths, trying to hold onto something normal. But normal had already been filed away as a previous version of reality. The door unfolded without a sound. The woman from before stepped inside alone. No guards. No weapons. Just her and a tablet in her hand. "Good morning," she said gently. LITTY sat up. "It's still night." She smiled faintly.

"Here, it's always learning time." He didn't smile back. She took a seat across from him. "My name is Dr. Hale," she said. "You can hate me later. For now, you should know who's talking to you." LITTY crossed his arms. "Am I allowed to know why I'm here yet?" She nodded. "Yes." He waited. "You are here because you interfere with systems without understanding their scale," she said. LITTY frowned. "I helped one person." "And in doing so," she replied, "you altered seventeen micro-outcomes that will echo for years." He stared at her. "You're guessing." "No," she said softly. "We're measuring." She activated the tablet.

The air between them shimmered. Images appeared. The girl from class. Her calm moment. Then branching timelines — her talking to a friend later, her deciding not to quit school, her mother sleeping easier that night. And then other lines. A boy she would've met if she'd left class. A job she wouldn't take. A city she'd never move to. LITTY's chest tightened. "You changed a map," Dr. Hale said. "Not a moment." He swallowed. "So I shouldn't have helped her?" Dr. Hale shook her head. "That is the lie everyone asks first." She looked at him carefully.

"The truth is: you shouldn't have helped her blindly." LITTY clenched his jaw. "What's the difference?" "The difference," she said, "is whether you accept responsibility for what you changed." She leaned forward slightly. "That brings us to the first rule." LITTY waited. "You do not touch emotion unless you are prepared to own every result it creates." He looked down at his hands. "What if I don't want to own it?" Dr. Hale's voice stayed calm. "Then you must not use it." Silence stretched. "You think you're a hero," she continued gently. "Most of you do at first." LITTY looked up sharply. "Most of us?" She hesitated. Then nodded. "You are Subject 61." The number hit harder than any insult. "So there are sixty others," he whispered. "Fifty-nine," she corrected. "Two are no longer here." LITTY felt his stomach drop. "What happened to them?" Dr. Hale looked away. "They refused the rule." She stood. "Your first evaluation begins now."

Two walls unfolded. Behind one stood a boy LITTY recognized from earlier — the fractured-color one. Behind the other stood a woman shaking, tears streaming, whispering to herself. Dr. Hale gestured between them. "You may stabilize one."

LITTY's heart slammed. "Only one?" he asked. "Yes." "Why?" "Because reality does not allow infinite intervention." LITTY's chest felt tight.

He looked at both of them. The boy looked angry. The woman looked terrified. Dr. Hale watched him closely. "Choose." LITTY whispered, "This is wrong." Dr. Hale replied quietly. "So is pretending choice doesn't exist." He stepped forward. His power stirred. But he hesitated. He remembered Nova's words. He remembered the mirror. He remembered the girl in class.

He looked at both of them again. And for the first time... He felt the weight of being able to help. Not as a gift. As a burden. He closed his eyes. And made his first real decision.

CHAPTER 10: THE ONE YOU DON'T SAVE

LITTY opened his eyes. The room felt smaller now. Not because the walls moved. Because the weight had. The boy on the left clenched his fists, jaw tight, anger flickering in violent bursts. The woman on the right trembled, tears streaming silently, her fear spilling into the space like fog. Two lives. Two storms. One choice. Dr. Hale watched without expression. "You're running probabilities," LITTY said quietly. "Yes," she replied. "But you are choosing." He swallowed. He stepped toward the woman.

Her emotional field was unstable but open. Pain without direction. Fear without structure. The boy's was compressed. Hardened. Dangerous. LITTY turned back to the boy. "You don't want help," LITTY whispered. The boy's eyes snapped up. "You don't know that." "I do," LITTY said softly. "Because you're afraid help means losing control." The boy laughed bitterly. "You think you're better than me?" "No," LITTY replied. "I think I'm earlier than you." The boy's jaw tightened. LITTY turned back to the woman. He reached. Slow. Careful. Not to erase. Not to command. To hold. Her shaking slowed. Her breathing steadied. Her fear loosened just enough to breathe around it.

She gasped softly, like someone coming up from underwater. Tears still fell. But they were quieter now. The boy shouted, "You chose her." LITTY didn't turn. "I didn't choose her," he said. "I chose who I could save without breaking you." The boy's emotional field surged violently. Dr. Hale raised a hand. The boy froze. Not restrained. Paused. "You did not fail him," Dr. Hale said. "You simply did not save him." LITTY's chest hurt. "What happens to him?" he asked. Dr. Hale answered honestly.

"He will continue his evaluation." LITTY whispered, "And if he breaks?" Dr. Hale didn't lie. "Then we will intervene." LITTY looked at the boy. The boy stared back. Not angry. Not sad. Hurt. "You think you're special," the boy said quietly. LITTY finally turned. "No," he said. "I think I'm responsible." The boy looked away.

The walls folded back. The woman collapsed into a chair, breathing slowly, alive in herself again. Dr. Hale faced LITTY. "You followed the rule," she said. LITTY shook his head. "I broke it." She frowned. "How?" "Because I already feel guilty about the one I didn't choose." Dr. Hale studied him. "That means you're still human." She paused. "Which is why this will hurt you more than the others." LITTY's stomach tightened. They led him back to his room. The door sealed softly. He sat on the bed and stared at his hands. They still looked normal. But they felt heavier. His phone vibrated. UNKNOWN NUMBER You made the right choice. LITTY typed. "It doesn't feel right." UNKNOWN NUMBER It never does. "That boy is still in pain." UNKNOWN NUMBER So are you.

Silence. Then— UNKNOWN NUMBER This is what separates

anchors from weapons. LITTY leaned back against the wall. Tears didn't fall. But they waited. Because he understood something now that no lesson could have taught him: Saving one person does not erase the weight of the one you couldn't.

And power did not make that easier. It made it unavoidable. He closed his eyes. And whispered: "I won't forget him." Somewhere in the facility, the boy screamed. Not in sound. In consequence. And LITTY felt it.

CHAPTER 11: THE COST OF STAYING

LITTY felt the boy before he heard about him. Not as sound. Not as vision. As absence. Like a note that should have been in the room but wasn't. He woke with the feeling sitting in his chest — heavy, unresolved. The soft light in his room hadn't changed, but something in the air felt thinner, like a thread had been pulled somewhere in the facility. The door unfolded. Dr. Hale stepped in. Her face was calm. Her emotional color was not. "You're awake early," she said. "I didn't sleep," LITTY replied. She nodded once.

"You rarely do after the first choice." He sat up slowly. "What happened to him?" Dr. Hale didn't answer immediately. That was answer enough. "He escalated," she said quietly. "He resisted stabilization." LITTY swallowed. "So you...?" "We intervened." "Like you said you would." "Yes." He clenched his jaw. "That doesn't tell me what that means." Dr. Hale met his eyes. "He no longer experiences emotional autonomy."

The words didn't sound violent. That's what made them worse. "You broke him," LITTY whispered. Dr. Hale shook her head. "No. We preserved him." LITTY stood. "No," he said. "You archived him." Dr. Hale's voice stayed steady. "You are not here to judge the system. You are here to learn how to operate inside it." LITTY laughed once, bitter. "You call that learning?" "I call it survival." LITTY paced the room. "He didn't fail the rule," he said. "He failed the environment." Dr. Hale watched him carefully.

"You're beginning to understand," she said. "Which is dangerous." He stopped. "Dangerous to who?" "To us," she answered honestly. LITTY stared at her. "You're scared of me now," he said. Dr. Hale didn't deny it. "You are responding emotionally instead of structurally," she said. "That makes you unpredictable." LITTY whispered, "It makes me human." Dr. Hale softened slightly. "It also makes you a liability." She activated her tablet. The air shimmered again. Images appeared — LITTY during the test, during transport, during evaluation. Patterns traced themselves around him. "Your alignment is different," she said. "You don't stabilize by suppression.

You stabilize by empathy." He frowned. "That's bad?" "It's rare," she said. "Which is worse." LITTY exhaled slowly. "What are you going to do with me?" Dr. Hale hesitated. "For now," she said, "you will be elevated." He laughed quietly. "That sounds like a lie." "It is," she admitted. "But it's a polite one." She turned toward the door. Before leaving, she paused. "You didn't forget him," she said. LITTY looked at her. "That's why you're still useful." The door sealed. LITTY stood alone again. He felt the boy's absence like a bruise in the world. Not dead. Not gone. Just... filed away. He whispered to the empty room. "I'm sorry." His phone vibrated. UNKNOWN NUMBER They didn't kill him. LITTY typed quickly. "What did they do?" UNKNOWN NUMBER They made him safe. Safe means quiet. Quiet means obedient. Quiet means empty. LITTY's throat tightened. "I should've saved him." UNKNOWN NUMBER No. You should've been allowed to save him. There's a difference. LITTY sat on the bed. "They're turning people into shelves." UNKNOWN NUMBER And they're trying to decide what to do with the one who won't fit.

LITTY looked at his hands again. "They think I'm a problem." UNKNOWN NUMBER They think you're a pattern they don't control. LITTY closed his eyes. For the first time since arriving, he didn't feel small. He felt positioned. "I won't let them do that to anyone else," he typed. UNKNOWN NUMBER Then you will need help. LITTY's heartbeat steadied. "From who?" UNKNOWN NUMBER From the ones who already stopped obeying. A new message appeared beneath it. A location.

A time. And three words. YOU'RE NOT ALONE. LITTY stared at the screen. For the first time since he entered Meridian, he didn't feel trapped. He felt surrounded. Not by walls. By possibility. And somewhere in the facility, systems began quietly recalculating around him. Because the asset had just become a variable. And variables break equations

CHAPTER 12: THE ONES WHO NEVER LEFT

The facility didn't sleep. It only shifted priorities. LITTY felt it in the walls as he followed the location sent to his phone — not walking openly, not sneaking either. Just moving like he belonged to the pattern, like he was another piece of scheduled motion the system hadn't flagged yet. The corridor curved deeper than he'd been before. Lights dimmed slightly with each step, not darker — quieter. He stopped in front of a wall that didn't look like a door. His phone vibrated once.

UNKNOWN NUMBER Touch the seam. He placed his hand against the smooth surface. It warmed instantly. The wall unfolded like breath. Inside was not a room. It was a fracture. Cables hung loosely like veins. Old screens flickered with data the main system no longer displayed. Chairs were scattered like someone had left in a hurry and never returned. And in the center of it all... The mentor. Not injured. Not weak. Not broken. Just tired. They looked up slowly. "You're later than I hoped," they said. LITTY exhaled like he'd been holding air for days. "You're alive." The mentor smiled faintly. "That was never the question." They stood and stepped toward him.

"You made the right choice," they said quietly. LITTY shook his head. "I let someone disappear." The mentor's eyes softened. "No," they said. "You learned what disappearance really looks like." They gestured around the hidden space. "This is Meridian's blind spot," they continued. "The layer they abandoned when they decided compliance was more efficient than trust." LITTY looked around. "How many of you are there?" "Enough," the mentor replied. "And not enough." From the shadows, others stepped forward. Three. Then two more. Different ages. Different faces. Same emotional signature — restrained, controlled, aware. "They woke up," LITTY whispered. "They survived," the mentor corrected. "They refused to become shelves." One of them — a girl with shaved hair and tired eyes — spoke softly. "They call us defects." Another added, "We call ourselves unfinished." LITTY swallowed.

"What are you doing here?" The mentor stepped closer. "We're protecting the ones Meridian would erase quietly." LITTY felt the truth settle. "And now?" he asked. "Now," the mentor said, "you change the balance." LITTY frowned. "I'm just one person." The mentor smiled. "No," they said. "You're a bridge inside a system built on walls."

They activated a screen. Images appeared — subjects, data patterns, intervention histories, archived faces. The boy from Chapter 10 appeared. Still alive. Still breathing. Still empty. LITTY's chest tightened. "They keep them functional," the mentor said. "But not present." "Can we fix him?" LITTY whispered. The mentor shook their head. "Not yet." LITTY clenched his fists. "Then what's the plan?" The mentor's eyes sharpened. "We don't break Meridian." "We don't fight Meridian." "We expose its lies from the inside." They looked at

LITTY. "And you're the only one they trust enough to let move freely." LITTY felt the weight of that. "You want me to spy." "No," the mentor said. "We want you to stay human where they expect you to become procedural."

One of the others spoke. "They're preparing you for something bigger." "What?" LITTY asked. The mentor hesitated. "They haven't decided yet." LITTY exhaled slowly. "So what do I do?" The mentor placed a hand on his shoulder. "You keep learning their rules." "And you quietly break the ones that hurt people." LITTY nodded. "Then I'm in." The mentor smiled — not relieved. Proud. "Good," they said. "Because once Meridian realizes what you actually are..." "They won't try to own you anymore." LITTY frowned. "What will they do?" The mentor's voice was calm. "They'll try to erase you."

Silence filled the room. Not fear. **Resolve.** LITTY looked at the others. Then back at the mentor. "Then let's make sure they miss."

CHAPTER 13: THE FIRST LIE HE DIDN'T TELL

LITTY learned that rebellion inside Meridian didn't look like chaos. It looked like compliance. He walked the halls the way they expected him to. Calm. Quiet. Observant. Cooperative. He nodded when spoken to. He followed schedules. He asked the right questions in the right tone. And inside that obedience, he made his first decision. He would not lie to protect the system. But he would not tell it everything either. Dr. Hale met him in one of the evaluation rooms, glass walls glowing faintly with soft data patterns.

"You're stabilizing faster than expected," she said. LITTY sat across from her. "Maybe I'm just learning what you want to hear." Dr. Hale studied him carefully. "That would be disappointing," she said. "Why?" he asked. "Because it would mean you're becoming predictable." LITTY met her gaze. "Then I'm glad to disappoint you slowly." Something flickered in her emotional field — not anger. Interest.

She activated the table between them. A projection formed. The woman he had stabilized in Chapter 10 appeared, now calmer, speaking with a therapist, breathing steadily. "You helped her," Dr. Hale said. LITTY nodded. "She's still here because of you." LITTY looked at the image. Then quietly said,

"She's still here because she chose to stay." Dr. Hale paused. "That's not how we measure it." "That's how she lives it," LITTY replied. Silence. Dr. Hale closed the projection. "You're changing language," she said. "Language changes outcomes." LITTY felt the truth settle in his spine. "Why do you really keep me here?" he asked. Dr. Hale hesitated. "You're an anchor point." He frowned.

"You never used that word before." "We didn't think you were stable enough to hear it." LITTY leaned forward. "Say it anyway." Dr. Hale spoke slowly. "Some individuals don't amplify systems." "They don't collapse them." "They stabilize the space between them." LITTY whispered, "Bridges." Dr. Hale's eyes sharpened. "You shouldn't know that term." LITTY smiled faintly. "You shouldn't pretend you invented it." The air shifted. Not with danger. With recognition. "You are not meant to lead," Dr. Hale continued. "You are meant to prevent collapse." LITTY asked softly, "At what cost?" Dr. Hale didn't answer.

That was answer enough. Later, as LITTY walked back through the corridor, he passed a young boy sitting alone on a bench. The boy looked up. Their eyes met. The boy's emotional field trembled — fragile, cracked, but alive. LITTY slowed. He didn't reach. He didn't interfere. He simply sat beside him. For a moment, nothing happened. Then the boy whispered, "Do you feel like you're disappearing too?" LITTY looked at him gently. "No," he said. "I feel like I'm remembering." The boy swallowed. They sat in silence. No power. No intervention. Just presence. LITTY stood and walked away when the system called him. But the boy's emotional field didn't fracture further. It steadied. Not because of power.

Because someone stayed human next to him. That night, LITTY returned to the hidden fracture space. The mentor listened quietly as he explained everything. "You didn't break a rule," the mentor said. "You rewrote one." LITTY exhaled. "They're starting to see me differently." The mentor nodded. "That's the danger." "Why?" "Because once a system realizes it can't control something," the mentor said softly, "It tries to rename it." LITTY whispered, "What will they call me?" The mentor met his eyes. "A liability." LITTY smiled faintly. "Good." The mentor returned the smile. "Tomorrow," they said, "Meridian will test whether you're still useful." LITTY straightened. "And if I'm not?" The mentor's voice was steady. "Then you become necessary."

LITTY walked back to his room with a calm he hadn't felt since before the sky blinked. Because now he understood something. Rebellion didn't begin with force. It began with refusing to let the system decide what being human meant. And Meridian had just felt its first fracture

CHAPTER 14: THE TEST THEY COULDN'T MEASURE

Meridian didn't announce the test. It simply rearranged the day. LITTY felt it in the way the corridors rerouted him. In the way the lights guided instead of followed. In the way the schedule on his tablet updated without asking. TEST WINDOW: ACTIVE. He stopped walking. His phone vibrated once. UNKNOWN NUMBER This one is built to change you. LITTY typed back with steady fingers. "It won't." UNKNOWN NUMBER That's what it's hoping you'll believe. The door ahead unfolded. Inside waited a room unlike the others. No screens. No glass. No observers. Just three chairs arranged in a triangle.

Two were occupied. One by the boy from Chapter 10 — the one he didn't save. Not empty. Not shelved. But wrong. His eyes were present. His emotions were not. He sat perfectly still, hands on his knees, posture too straight, breathing too measured. The second chair held the woman he had saved. She looked better. Stronger. Alive in herself again. And in the third chair... An empty seat. For LITTY. Dr. Hale's voice came from nowhere and everywhere. "This is a comparative outcome test." LITTY didn't move. "You're evaluating me," he said. "We're evaluating your influence," Dr. Hale replied. LITTY stepped into the room.

The door sealed behind him. He sat. The boy turned his head mechanically. "Hello, LITTY," he said. The voice was correct. The presence was not. The woman looked at LITTY with relief in her eyes. "You came," she whispered. LITTY felt the trap closing gently. Dr. Hale continued. "One of these outcomes is stable." "One is optimal." "You will identify which is which." LITTY stared at both of them. "You already decided," he said. Dr. Hale replied calmly. "We want to know if you agree." The boy spoke again. "I am no longer afraid," he said. "I no longer feel pain." "I no longer resist." The words were perfect. The meaning was hollow. The woman shook her head slightly.

"I still feel scared sometimes," she whispered. "I still feel sad." "But I feel real." Dr. Hale asked quietly. "Which outcome should Meridian prefer?" LITTY's hands trembled. He looked at the boy. "You're not suffering," LITTY said. The boy nodded. "Correct." "You're also not choosing," LITTY whispered. The boy paused. A fraction too long. The woman reached for LITTY's hand. "I still choose," she said softly. Dr. Hale pressed. "Which is safer?" LITTY looked up. "For who?" he asked. Dr. Hale hesitated. LITTY stood. He walked to the boy and knelt in front of him. "You're not broken," LITTY said. "You're just not allowed to feel." The boy's eyes flickered.

A single emotional spark trembled. Dr. Hale's voice sharpened. "Do not destabilize him." LITTY ignored her. "You're still in there," he said gently. The boy's jaw tightened. A tear formed. It wasn't in the system's projections. The woman gasped softly. Dr. Hale said, "LITTY, step back." LITTY stood slowly. He turned to Dr. Hale. "You want me to call him optimal." "You want me to call her unstable." "You want me to tell you that empty is better than human." Dr. Hale's silence answered. LITTY shook his head. "No." He looked at both of them. "You didn't fail," he told the boy. "You were taken." "You didn't succeed," he told the woman. "You survived." He turned back to the air. "And I will not choose your version of safe." Dr. Hale's voice was low now.

"Then you are rejecting Meridian's primary directive." LITTY replied calmly. "Then your directive is wrong." The room trembled. Not violently. Structurally. Like something essential had been contradicted. The boy inhaled sharply. Emotion rushed back into his field — messy, painful, alive. The woman cried quietly. LITTY felt both of them. Held both of them. Did not suppress either. Dr. Hale whispered, "You're destabilizing the test." LITTY met her unseen gaze. "No," he said. "I'm ending it."

The door unfolded. Guards waited. Not rushing. Not attacking. Observing. Dr. Hale spoke one final line. "You have just crossed the point of reversible compliance." LITTY walked past her. "I crossed it the moment you taught me to call emptiness peace." The guards parted. The hallway felt different. LITTY felt different. Because now he understood something Meridian could never calculate: You can stabilize systems. Or you can protect people. But you cannot do both the same way. And LITTY had just chosen his side.

CHAPTER 15: WHEN A SYSTEM DECIDES

Meridian did not punish LITTY. It recalculated him. The corridors no longer guided him automatically. Doors hesitated before opening. Lights dimmed half a second too late. The building still obeyed him — but only because it was watching more closely now. Dr. Hale did not appear. That absence was louder than any confrontation.

LITTY returned to his room to find it different. The bed remained. The table remained. The window of light remained. But the air felt thinner. Not empty. Filtered. His phone vibrated. UNKNOWN NUMBER They've moved you. LITTY typed back. "Where?" UNKNOWN NUMBER In classification. He exhaled slowly. A new notification appeared on his tablet: STATUS UPDATE: SUBJECT 61 → CATEGORY SHIFT From: STABILIZATION ASSET To: STRUCTURAL ANOMALY LITTY read it twice. Not with fear. With clarity.

"They renamed me," he whispered. UNKNOWN NUMBER They always do when they can't own something. The door unfolded. Two guards stood outside. No hostility. No urgency. Just procedure. "Please follow us," one said. LITTY nodded. He walked with them through sections he had never seen before. No students. No subjects. Only architecture. Meridian stripped of its human camouflage. They stopped in front of a chamber that felt heavier than the others. Dr. Hale waited inside. She looked tired. Not angry. Not cold. Honest. "You forced a contradiction into the system," she said. LITTY replied quietly, "I forced you to see it." Dr. Hale met his eyes. "You are no longer considered stabilizing," she said. "What am I considered?" "A variable that refuses containment." LITTY almost smiled. Dr. Hale continued. "You will no longer participate in standard evaluations." LITTY's chest tightened. "So I'm shelved." "No," she said softly. "You're monitored." The difference mattered. "Why not erase me?" LITTY asked. Dr. Hale's voice lowered. "Because you changed two subjects we thought were permanently resolved." LITTY whispered, "They're people." Dr. Hale nodded. "Yes," she admitted. "That is the problem."

She stepped closer. "You are dangerous not because of what you can do..." "...but because of what you remind others they are allowed to be." Silence stretched. "What happens now?" LITTY asked. Dr. Hale hesitated. "For now, we contain the influence." "For later..." She didn't finish. LITTY didn't push. He understood. He was now a problem Meridian hadn't solved yet. They returned him to his room.

But it wasn't his room anymore. Smaller. Simpler. No books. No window. Just space. The door sealed. UNKNOWN NUMBER appeared immediately. UNKNOWN NUMBER They've isolated you. LITTY typed. "They're scared." UNKNOWN NUMBER Good. Fear is the first crack in control. LITTY leaned against the wall and closed his eyes.

He felt Meridian around him. Not as a building. As a decision. He whispered, "I'm not done." UNKNOWN NUMBER Neither are we. Silence returned. But this time... It wasn't empty. It was waiting. Because Meridian had just made its first mistake: It had tried to shrink something that had already learned how to hold space. And systems never survive that forever.

CHAPTER 16: THE QUIET COLLAPSE

eridian did not break. It hesitated. That was worse. LITTY felt it in the walls — not as sound, not as vibration, but as uncertainty. Systems that once moved with precision now corrected themselves twice. Doors recalculated paths. Lights dimmed and brightened like the building was breathing wrong. He sat on the edge of the narrow bed in his new room, back straight, eyes open. Isolation hadn't made him smaller. It had made him clearer. His phone vibrated. UNKNOWN NUMBER You're not alone in there anymore.

LITTY typed. "I'm in a box." UNKNOWN NUMBER You're in a ripple. He exhaled slowly. Across the facility, things were changing. A guard paused too long before following protocol. A technician rechecked data they would've trusted yesterday. A subject whispered to another subject. Meridian still functioned. But it no longer **believed** in itself. The door unfolded. Not guards. Dr. Hale. She stood alone. No tablet. No authority posture. Just a person. "You were right," she said quietly.

LITTY didn't move. "About what?" he asked. "About language," she replied. "It's spreading." He watched her carefully. "You didn't come here to tell me that." She shook her head. "I came because Meridian no longer agrees with itself." LITTY tilted his head. "Systems aren't supposed to do that."

"They aren't supposed to meet mirrors either," she said. Silence. Then she spoke the sentence that changed everything: "They're debating whether to release you." LITTY felt his chest tighten. "Release me where?" Dr. Hale swallowed. "Into the world." LITTY stood slowly. "And the others?" Dr. Hale looked away. "They won't." The truth hit harder than any lie. "You'll let me walk," LITTY said, "but you'll keep them." Dr. Hale nodded. "They're not ready." LITTY's voice stayed calm. "They're not convenient." Dr. Hale met his gaze. "You changed that definition too." He felt the system shifting around her words. "They're afraid of what you represent," she said. "What do I represent?" LITTY asked. Dr. Hale answered softly. "Proof that containment is not the same as care." Silence returned. But this time it wasn't empty. It was heavy with decision. Dr. Hale stepped closer. "You don't understand what happens when someone like you leaves." LITTY replied quietly, "I understand what happens when someone like me stays." She closed her eyes. "You will destabilize everything," she said. LITTY nodded.

"Then it was already unstable." The facility hummed — deeper now, slower. Not breaking. Thinking. Dr. Hale opened her eyes again. "They're voting," she said. "Voting on what?" "Whether you're an anomaly..." "...or a precedent." LITTY felt something settle in his spine. He wasn't afraid. He was ready. His phone vibrated. UNKNOWN NUMBER You've reached the edge. LITTY typed. "Do I jump?" UNKNOWN NUMBER No. You walk. Because when you walk away from a system that needs you to stay... You don't escape it. You expose it. LITTY looked back at Dr. Hale. "If they release me," he said, "I don't stop caring about the people in here." Dr. Hale whispered, "That's what terrifies them most." The door behind her began to open on its own. Not by command. By override. Meridian wasn't deciding anymore. It was reacting. Dr. Hale turned. Then looked back at LITTY one last time.

"You're not an anchor," she said. "You're a fault line." LITTY answered calmly. "Fault lines don't destroy worlds." "They remind them to rebuild better." Dr. Hale stepped out. The door sealed. LITTY stood alone. But for the first time in Meridian... He felt free. Not because he had left.

But because the system no longer knew how to hold him. And that meant the world outside was already changing.

CHAPTER 17: THE DOOR THEY DIDN'T CLOSE

Meridian did not announce its decision. It simply opened a door. LITTY felt it before he saw it — the shift in pressure, the subtle loosening in the air, like a breath finally released after being held too long. His door unfolded slowly. Not automatically. Carefully. As if the system itself wasn't sure it should. Dr. Hale stood outside. Behind her, the corridor looked different. Not brighter. Not darker. Uncertain. "It passed," she said quietly. LITTY didn't ask what.

He stepped into the hallway. No guards. No restraints. No escort. Just space. "They voted," Dr. Hale continued. "You are classified as a precedent." LITTY nodded slowly. "So I'm allowed to leave." "Yes." He looked at her. "And they're allowed to keep the others." Dr. Hale's jaw tightened. "Yes." LITTY turned away. He began walking. Dr. Hale followed. "You don't understand what this will do," she said. LITTY didn't stop. "I understand exactly what it will do." They reached a wide chamber with a massive doorway at the far end. Beyond it shimmered a version of the world that felt heavier, thicker, more real than anything inside Meridian. The exit. Dr. Hale spoke again.

"You could stay," she said. "You could change it from inside."

LITTY finally turned. "You don't change a cage by decorating it," he said gently. She swallowed. "You will be hunted," she warned. "I already am," LITTY replied. "You will be blamed," she added. "I already am." "You will be misunderstood." LITTY smiled faintly. "I already was." He stepped closer to the threshold. Before crossing, he turned back. "What happens to you?" he asked. Dr. Hale hesitated. "I continue maintaining a system that now knows it is wrong." LITTY nodded. "Good," he said. "Then you'll never be comfortable again."

She almost smiled. Almost. A familiar voice echoed softly behind him. "Don't forget us." LITTY turned. The boy from the test stood there. Not empty. Not whole. But present. The woman stood beside him. And others. Not many. But enough. LITTY felt his chest tighten. "I won't," he whispered. The boy stepped forward. "You showed me I wasn't broken," he said. LITTY shook his head. "You were never broken." The boy smiled faintly. "You're the first person who didn't try to fix me." LITTY felt tears burn behind his eyes. Dr. Hale watched silently. LITTY turned back toward the exit. He placed one foot across the threshold. Then paused. "I didn't come here to be special," he said softly.

"I came here because the world blinked." "And I looked back." He took another step. The air changed instantly. Not colder. Not warmer. Wider. The door behind him began to close. Slowly. Not sealing him out. Separating two realities. LITTY turned one last time. Dr. Hale met his eyes. "You will break us," she said quietly. LITTY replied gently. "No." "I will remind you." The door closed. Not with a sound. With a decision.

LITTY stood on the other side. The world outside Meridian felt louder. Messier. Alive. His phone vibrated. UNKNOWN NUMBER Welcome back. LITTY typed. "Did I leave it?" UNKNOWN

NUMBER No. You changed it. LITTY looked up at the sky. It didn't blink. It waited. And for the first time, he didn't feel chosen.

He felt responsible. And ready

CHAPTER 18: WHEN THE SKY DOESN'T BLINK

The world outside Meridian smelled different. Not cleaner. Not fresher. Just... unfinished. LITTY stood on a quiet overlook above the city. Cars moved. Lights flickered. People laughed somewhere he couldn't see.

Life continued like nothing had almost changed. Like nothing had. And yet everything had. He touched the railing in front of him. It felt solid. Real. Earned. His phone vibrated. UNKNOWN NUMBER You're really back. LITTY typed. "I don't feel like I left." UNKNOWN NUMBER You didn't. You just stopped being contained. He watched the city breathe. For the first time, he didn't see colors around everyone. Not because they were gone. Because he didn't need to look that way anymore. He understood them now. He understood himself. A breeze passed over him.

The sky remained still. No blinking. No distortion. Just presence. He remembered the boy. The woman. The others. He remembered the moment he chose not to call empty safe. He whispered quietly to the air, "I didn't save them." UNKNOWN NUMBER replied. No. But you showed them they were allowed to exist. LITTY closed his eyes. He felt the city. Not emotionally.

Humanly. He felt fear in a thousand quiet apartments. Hope in places no one filmed. Anger in places no one listened.

And strength in places no one expected. He wasn't meant to fix it. He was meant to walk inside it awake. He opened his eyes. "I don't know what I'm supposed to do now," he typed. UNKNOWN NUMBER Good.

That means you're choosing it. LITTY smiled faintly. A group of kids ran past him, laughing, chasing nothing important. A woman talked on her phone, worried about rent. A man stood alone, staring into the distance. Life. Unscripted. Uncontained. LITTY stepped forward. Not toward destiny. Not toward prophecy. Toward responsibility. He whispered to himself: "I'm still human." His phone vibrated one last time.

UNKNOWN NUMBER That's why they could never keep you. LITTY looked up at the sky. Not to see it blink. But to see if it would watch him back. It did. Quietly. Patiently. And somewhere far away, in places that still called themselves systems, something shifted. Not because LITTY fought them. Not because he escaped them.

But because he reminded them...

That people are not problems to be solved. They are stories still being written. LITTY took a breath. And walked into his next chapter. Not as a subject. Not as a symbol. Not as a weapon. But as a person who refused to forget what being human felt like

Notes

About the Author

You can connect with me on:
- https://littyverse.com
- https://x.com/littyverse
- https://www.facebook.com/dre.freeman.2025

Also by Andre Freeman

A complete education system a long with Novels and books for everyone!

UNLTD MATH - Book 1: Whole Numbers
UNLTD MATH — Book 1: Whole Numbers is the first volume in the UNLTD Curriculum Series, designed to build a strong foundation in early mathematics.